STAR WARS®

THE CLONE WARS™

CAPTURED

Adapted by Rob Valois

Based on the TV series *STAR WARS: THE CLONE WARS*

Grosset & Dunlap • LucasBooks

GROSSET & DUNLAP
Published by the Penguin Group
Penguin Group (USA) Inc., 375 Hudson Street, New York, New York 10014, USA
Penguin Group (Canada), 90 Eglinton Avenue East, Suite 700,
Toronto, Ontario M4P 2Y3, Canada
(a division of Pearson Penguin Canada Inc.)
Penguin Books Ltd., 80 Strand, London WC2R 0RL, England
Penguin Group Ireland, 25 St. Stephen's Green, Dublin 2, Ireland
(a division of Penguin Books Ltd.)
Penguin Group (Australia), 250 Camberwell Road, Camberwell, Victoria 3124,
Australia
(a division of Pearson Australia Group Pty. Ltd.)
Penguin Books India Pvt. Ltd., 11 Community Centre, Panchsheel Park,
New Delhi—110 017, India
Penguin Group (NZ), 67 Apollo Drive, Rosedale, North Shore 0632, New Zealand
(a division of Pearson New Zealand Ltd.)
Penguin Books (South Africa) (Pty.) Ltd., 24 Sturdee Avenue,
Rosebank, Johannesburg 2196, South Africa

Penguin Books Ltd., Registered Offices:
80 Strand, London WC2R 0RL, England

This book is published in partnership with LucasBooks, a division of Lucasfilm Ltd.

The publisher does not have any control over and does not assume any responsibility
for author or third-party websites or their content.

Library of Congress Cataloging-in-Publication Data is available.

ISBN 978-0-448-45202-9   10 9 8 7 6 5 4 3 2 1

GLOSSARY

Here are some *Clone Wars* terms that might help you along the way.

Blaster: The main weapon used in the galaxy.

Clone troopers: Biologically identical soldiers bred and trained to serve in the Galactic Republic's army.

Coruscant: The capital of the galaxy and home of the Jedi Council.

The Force: An energy field created by all living things. It gives the Jedi their power.

Galactic Republic: The government that rules the galaxy.

Hologram: A projected image of a person.

Jedi: Masters of the Force. They use their power to protect the Republic.

Jedi Council: The group of twelve Jedi Masters who oversee all the Jedi in the galaxy.

Lightsaber: The weapon of a Jedi. It looks like a sword made of colored energy.

Outer Rim: A wild and lawless part of the galaxy.

Parsec: A measurement of distance.

Separatist Alliance: The group trying to take over the Galactic Republic.

Sith Lords: Masters of the dark side of the Force and the enemy of the Jedi.

Vulture droids: Large ships that can turn into walking droids.

CHAPTER 1

After a long and difficult search, the Jedi
had tracked the Sith Lord Count Dooku to a
Separatist battle cruiser in the Outer Rim of
the galaxy. Jedi Knight Anakin Skywalker
allowed himself to be captured in order to get
aboard the ship and disable the cruiser's security
system. Once disabled, Jedi Master Obi-Wan
Kenobi was able to sneak aboard through a
maintenance hatch.

Obi-Wan dropped from the hatch into a hallway that was heavily patrolled by battle droid guards. He snuck past the guards and made his way toward the prison cell where Anakin was being held. When he opened the door, Anakin was gone.

Just then, a shadowy figure dropped from the ceiling. Obi-Wan ignited his lightsaber and spun around, ready to attack, but saw that the figure was his friend, Anakin.

"This is how you thank me for rescuing you?"

Obi-Wan said. "Pounce from the ceiling?"

Anakin smiled as Obi-Wan reached into his robe and pulled out another lightsaber. Anakin reached out his hand and the lightsaber flew through the air to him. The power of the Force allows Jedi to move objects with their minds.

"Thanks," Anakin said as he held his lightsaber in his hand.

"Did you manage to locate Dooku before landing in jail?" Obi-Wan asked.

"I know that he's onboard," Anakin replied.

Count Dooku sat alone in his chamber, his eyes closed. He was meditating.

"Obi-Wan Kenobi," he said with his eyes still closed. "I thought I sensed an unpleasant disturbance in the Force."

Jedi and Sith are able to use the power of the Force to sense one another. It makes it very difficult for them to sneak up on one another.

Dooku opened his eyes. Obi-Wan and Anakin stood at the doorway, their lightsabers lit and ready for action.

Just then, the ship rocked. It was under attack. A hologram of the droid pilot appeared.

"Sir . . ." it said. "It appears that there's a Jedi cruiser attacking."

Anakin smiled and stepped toward Dooku. "Your ship is surrounded, Count," he said. "Republic troops are boarding as we speak."

"You're to be taken to Coruscant," Obi-Wan added. "Where you'll stand trial before the Senate."

"Jedi fools . . ." Dooku sneered at them as the floor below him opened. He dropped through and escaped.

"I should have seen that coming," Obi-Wan said as he shook his head.

"Yeah," Anakin replied. "You should have."

CHAPTER 2

Count Dooku slid out of a tube in the ceiling and landed gracefully in the ship's hangar, where smaller shuttle crafts were kept. Two battle droids greeted him.

"Your ship is ready, sir," one of the droids said.

Obi-Wan ran into the hangar and saw Count Dooku climb aboard his ship. He charged forward, but the battle droids blocked his way.

With his lightsaber, he chopped the droids in half. There was an attack shuttle nearby. He quickly climbed into it and fired up the engines. Anakin charged into the room and scrambled onboard.

Being a better pilot, Anakin took the controls of the shuttle from Obi-Wan. The ship blasted out after Count Dooku.

Obi-Wan hit a button on the control panel and the ship's weapons came online. He kept firing until one of the laser blasts blew a hole in Dooku's ship. The ship began smoking as it spiraled off toward the planet below.

"That was easy," Anakin said to Obi-Wan.

"Lucky for you," Obi-Wan smiled back, "I'm an excellent shot."

Just then a vulture droid appeared and opened fire on Anakin and Obi-Wan's ship. Anakin tried to dodge the laser blasts, but they came too fast. Their ship was on fire and began to fall toward the blue planet below.

"Lucky for you," Anakin said as the ship shook around them, "I'm an excellent pilot."

"So you keep saying . . ." Obi-Wan replied as he braced himself for a crash landing.

The shuttle's landing gear opened, but the ship was moving so fast that Anakin couldn't get it to

stop. The ship bounced and spun and eventually slid to a stop right next to Dooku's shuttle, which had crashed on the planet as well.

The two Jedi were searching the crash site for Dooku when they came to the mouth of a large cave. Anakin got a serious look on his face and pulled out his lightsaber.

"You sense it, too," Obi-Wan said to Anakin. "There are many life-forms in there."

"And Dooku's one of them," Anakin added as

he ignited his lightsaber and entered the cave.

Anakin paused as they entered a large room. He sensed something and turned quickly. At that moment, a thundering sound filled the room.

"What is that?" Obi-Wan asked.

But before Anakin could answer, an avalanche of rocks rained down on top of the two Jedi, burying them completely.

Standing on the ledge above them was Count Dooku. He had caused the avalanche.

CHAPTER 3

Dooku jumped down from the ledge as the dust settled to the ground. He walked around the pile of rocks until he noticed something in the rubble. He kicked a few rocks aside and saw Anakin's lightsaber.

"You won't be needing this anymore, Skywalker," he said as he picked up the lightsaber and put it in his robe.

The Sith Lord laughed as he walked out of

the cavernous room. He turned and paused for a moment before raising his hands in the air. The ceiling of the cave began to shake and rumble. Small rocks fell to the ground, and then larger ones crashed down. Dooku used the Force to seal off the entrance to the cave.

Dooku made his way across the rugged blue and green terrain toward his abandoned ship. As he came to a small hill, he stopped. Another ship

had landed next to his abandoned shuttle and Anakin and Obi-Wan's crashed ship.

A bunch of angry-looking space pirates were swarming around the two vessels. They had stolen everything that they could and were tearing the ships to pieces for spare parts.

As the pirates worked, their leader stood watch over them. His name was Hondo. He was a humanoid with deeply tanned and rough, wrinkled skin. Dooku recognized him as a Weequay, a creature from the planet Sriluur in the Outer Rim.

A small monkeylike creature jumped from

one pirate's shoulder to the next until it finally
jumped up onto the back of the pirate leader.
Hondo turned to see Dooku walking toward
them.

"Well," he said. "What do we have here?"

"Who are you?" Dooku asked as he looked at
the damage to his ship.

"More importantly," the pirate replied, "who are you?"

The two men stood staring at each other.

"Your solar sailor is very beautiful," the pirate finally said. "A pretty expensive ship."

Dooku didn't say a word.

"What are you doing out here?" the pirate asked.

"I took some damage in an asteroid storm and had to make an emergency landing," Dooku replied. "Feel free to help yourself to it."

Hondo looked Dooku over. He could see the two lightsabers barely hidden under the Sith Lord's robe.

"If you need transport," the pirate added, "the nearest planet is Florrum. It's six parsecs away."

"Is it civilized?" Dooku asked.

"Depends on your definition of civilized," he replied. "But you'd certainly be more comfortable there than here."

"Perhaps I'll take you up on your offer," Dooku said, agreeing to let the pirates fly him off of the planet.

CHAPTER 4

The pirates' ship touched down on the planet Florrum in a large plaza where all types of ships were parked. Surrounding the plaza were many fortresslike buildings. The ship's ramp lowered and Dooku emerged to find an army of tanks, and pirates, all with their weapons pointed at him.

"Welcome to Florrum," Hondo smirked as he exited the ship.

Dooku reached for his lightsaber, but it was missing.

"Are these what you're looking for, Jedi?" Hondo asked as he waved the two lightsabers at Dooku.

"I am more powerful than any Jedi," Dooku threatened.

"Then you must be worth more, too," the pirate added.

"Know that you are dealing with a Sith Lord," Dooku announced as he raised his hands and moved toward Hondo.

"But you're still outnumbered," Hondo said as the other pirates moved in around Dooku.

"The leader of the clanker army. And a Sith Lord no less." Hondo smiled. "Someone is sure to pay a pretty price for you."

"Provide me with the proper means of communication," Dooku submitted. "I will

arrange for any ransom to be paid."

Hondo shook his head. "And give you a chance to crush us? You don't survive in the Outer Rim by being stupid."

"If the Separatists will pay to get you back," he added, "chances are that the Republic will offer even more."

Dooku stood silently. He knew this was true.

CHAPTER 5

Back in the cave, the pile of rocks began to shudder and move. Then one giant boulder rose up and levitated above the pile. A figure began to crawl out. It was Anakin. He rolled down the side of the pile to the ground before the large boulder crashed back down.

Anakin quickly started to dig through the rubble. Obi-Wan was still buried under the rocks.

"Obi-Wan, can you hear me?" he called out.

He waited for a reply, but all that he could hear was the echo of his own voice in the cave. He reached for his lightsaber to cut through the rocks, but it was gone. He couldn't believe that he'd lost it.

"If there's one thing that I've tried to teach you," a voice called out from behind him.

Anakin spun around to see Obi-Wan entering the cave from a small side entrance.

"Master! You're alive!" Anakin said, happy to see his friend.

"You need to hang on to your lightsaber," the elder Jedi continued.

"It got knocked out of my hand," Anakin replied.

"By a rock?" Obi-Wan asked.

"Yeah, by a rock," Anakin answered.

Obi-Wan and Anakin struggled to clear the debris from the cave entrance. Then, as if by magic, the wall of boulders and debris exploded.

The two Jedi were blinded by the bright sunlight. By the time they knew what was happening, they were surrounded by clone troopers. Reinforcements had arrived.

The space pirates had contacted the Jedi
Council and Hondo told Yoda that he would give
Count Dooku to them for a million credits. Yoda
knew that they needed to capture Dooku, so
he sent Anakin and Obi-Wan to meet with the
pirates. He wanted them to make sure that the
pirates really had Dooku.

On the planet Florrum, Anakin and Obi Wan
met with Hondo and his pirate crew. There was
a massive party in the main hall of the pirates'
base. They were celebrating the ransom that they
would be getting for turning Dooku over to the
Republic.

"Can I persuade you to join us for a drink?" Hondo asked the two Jedi.

Anakin and Obi-Wan exchanged a look. They didn't trust the pirates.

"It's a tradition," Hondo added. "In the name of friendship!"

While the pirates were distracted, Obi-Wan and Anakin used the Force to switch their drinks with the drinks of two pirates that were seated near them. They were afraid that the pirates might have put drugs in their drinks.

"To our new friends, the Republic!" Hondo cheered.

Anakin and Obi-Wan smiled at each other as they sipped their drinks.

CHAPTER 6

The next thing that Obi-Wan knew, he was in a prison cell and Anakin was asleep on the cot next to him. They both had braceletlike binders on their wrists that prevented them from using the Force and they were tied together with a long cord. Obi-Wan looked around. He was not sure where his was. He shook Anakin awake.

"Master? What happened?" Anakin asked.

"We were drugged," Obi-Wan answered.

"A shrewd observation, Master Kenobi," said Dooku. He was on the cot just next to them.

The same cord that bound Anakin and Obi-Wan together was also connected to Dooku.

"Well, since we're all tied together," Obi-Wan said. "It looks like we should try to work together."

Dooku didn't like the idea of working with the Jedi, but he had tried every way to escape, and he knew that he needed their help.

"So . . ." Dooku said. "Have you two come up with any brilliant ideas?"

"I'm working on it," Obi-Wan replied. He didn't have a plan.

Then Dooku saw what he was waiting for. One of the pirates had left a plate and knife on a table on the other side of the room.

Dooku reached his hand through the energy bars of the cell and began to concentrate. The binders made it very hard, but eventually he was able to use the Force to pull the knife into the cell. With the Force, he was able to use the knife to jimmy the lock. The energy bars dissolved and they were free.

"Well done," Dooku smiled. "If I do say so myself."

"Most impressive," Obi-Wan admitted.

The three of them moved out of the cell. They were still tied together.

"We do know where we're going, don't we?" Anakin asked.

"Hush, Anakin," Obi-Wan said. There was a pirate coming right toward them.

Dooku swung his arm and knocked the pirate to the ground. Anakin searched the body and found a key card.

"This is the way to the hangar," Dooku said as he pointed to a locked door.

Anakin slipped the key card into the control panel and the door slid open. There were four pirates on the other side with their blasters pointed at them.

CHAPTER 7

Anakin, Obi-Wan, and Dooku found themselves back in the prison cell.

"What are we doing following a Sith Lord?" Anakin asked.

Obi-Wan was busy with the pirate guard who stood outside their cell.

"You do not want to stand guard," Obi-Wan said as he waved his hand in front of the guard's face. He was using a Jedi mind trick on the guard.

"I do not want to be a guard," the pirate replied. His eyes had gone glassy.

"You want to deactivate the cell bars," Obi-Wan continued.

"I . . . I . . . want . . . to . . ." the pirate resisted.

Obi-Wan tried again. "You want to deactivate the cell bars and . . . go play cards."

The guard smiled. The mind trick worked.

"I want to deactivate the cell bars and go play cards," he said as he hit a button on the control panel.

The bars dissolved and once again Obi-Wan, Anakin, and Dooku were free. They could see the shadows of more pirates coming their way.

"Hurry up, Dooku!" Obi-Wan called to the Sith Lord.

"You should be more patient, Master," Anakin said. "After all, the Count is an elderly gentleman and doesn't move like he used to."

"I suppose you're right," Obi-Wan smiled.

Dooku gave them both an angry look. "I would kill you both right now," he said. "But then I'd have to drag your bodies around."

The shadows got closer. The three captives ran

through a maze of hallways until they reached the edge of the compound.

"We just have to get over that wall," Obi-Wan said as he pointed to the massive outer wall of the pirates' fortress.

Anakin jumped up and was able to get his fingertips over the top of the wall. Obi-Wan and Dooku hung below him on the cord. Anakin used his strength to pull them both up as the pirates' blaster fire hit the wall around them.

Just then, a blaster bolt hit the cord between Obi-Wan and Dooku, cutting it in half. Obi-Wan quickly reach out and grabbed Dooku's hand, keeping him from falling.

Anakin used all his strength to pull all three of them to the top of the wall. But when they got there they saw Hondo and his guards.

CHAPTER 8

A Republic shuttle prepared to land on Florrum.
Jar Jar Binks had been sent to deliver the ransom
for Count Dooku. He had no idea that Anakin and
Obi-Wan had been captured. But before the shuttle
could land, another group of pirates attacked it,
trying to steal the ransom for themselves.

The shuttle crashed on the planet's surface.
Jar Jar and the clone troopers had to finish their
mission on foot.

"How do we know where the pirate base is?" one of the clone troopers asked.

"Well, look at that," Commander Stone said as he pointed to a row of poles with power lines running across them.

"Theresa power, deresa be people, too," Jar Jar said. He knew that if they followed the power lines they'd get to the pirates' base.

Jar Jar and the clones made their way toward the pirate base.

"There be some bombat clankers comin' thisa way," Jar Jar called out when he saw pirates on speeder bikes and a giant tank coming toward them.

The clone soldiers readied their weapons as Jar Jar went to meet the pirates. It was his job to negotiate with them.

"What are you supposed to be?" a pirate asked as he saw Jar Jar approaching.

"Meesa Representative Binks," Jar Jar said. "Meesa comin' to deliver the ransom."

"If he's a Representative," the pirate called to his friends, "then he might be worth something as well."

"Sir, they're taking Representative Binks hostage," one of the clone troopers reported.

"Hopefully the pirates will take the bait," Commander Stone replied.

"Sir?" the clone trooper asked. He didn't know what the commander meant.

The pirates led Jar Jar into the tank. Just then, he tripped and hit the controls. The tank spun wildly. He tried to hit the ignition switch to stop it from spinning, but hit the accelerator instead. The tank moved at full speed and crashed into one of the power poles. The pole fell to the ground and knocked out all the power to the pirates' base.

CHAPTER 9

To keep an eye on the two Jedi, Hondo suspended Anakin and Obi-Wan in midair in the compound's main hall, their hands and feet bound by electric fields. They couldn't move at all.

Dooku was back in the prison cell under constant guard. Hondo was waiting on the ransom money and couldn't risk letting him escape again.

Suddenly, the hall went dark. With no power, Anakin and Obi-Wan were free. Anakin quickly dove at Hondo and knocked him to the floor. He used the Force to retrieve his lightsaber from the pirate's belt. He ignited it and pointed it right at Hondo.

"What chance do you have, Jedi?" Hondo said. "Let me go, and I may let you live."

Anakin looked up to see a swarm of pirates coming toward him.

Obi-Wan called out, "We must get to the landing area."

"If any of you approach us," Anakin yelled to the pirates as he pressed his lightsaber against Hondo, "he gets it."

Obi-Wan, Anakin, and Hondo made their way to the landing area. Hondo laughed as he saw one of his tanks rolling toward them. He thought that it was his men coming to rescue him. But then the tank stopped and Jar Jar popped out of the top.

"Ani! Obi!" Jar Jar called out. "Meesa arrived with the ransom!"

"Excellent, Jar Jar," Obi-Wan smiled. "That is assuming that the pirates still have Dooku to trade."

Just then, a pirate shuttle launched into the sky. It was Count Dooku. He had escaped!

"Well," Anakin said. "That answers that question."

"So, what now, Jedi?" Hondo asked Obi-Wan. "You going to arrest me and bring me to justice?"

"No," Obi-Wan replied. "Anakin, release him."

"What?!" Anakin screamed. He couldn't

believe that Obi-Wan wanted to let this pirate
go free.

"Hondo, you have nothing that we want,"
Obi-Wan explained. "And since we are no longer
prisoners, you have no bargaining power."

"Hold on," the pirate said. "After everything,
you're just going to let me walk away."

"We have no quarrel with you and we seek
no revenge," the Jedi added. "However, you'll
find that Count Dooku does not share our sense

of honor. And he now knows where you live."

Obi-Wan smiled at Anakin. They did not capture Count Dooku, but they knew that they would have other chances.